The ABC Book
of Australian Poetry

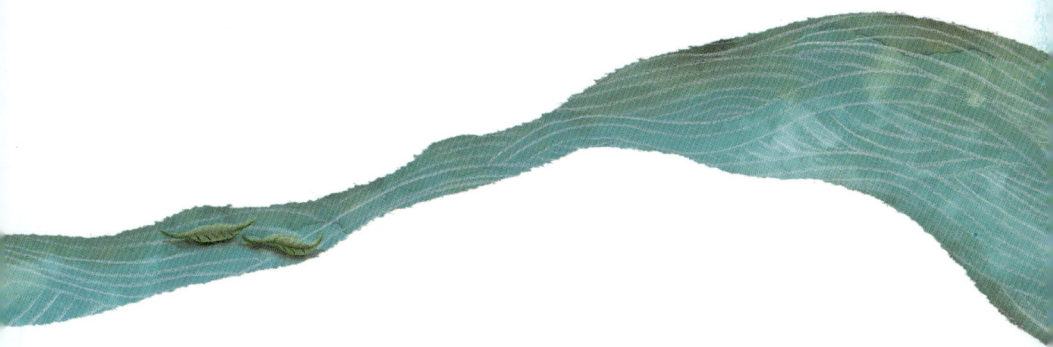

The ABC Book of Australian Poetry

A treasury of poems for young people

compiled by Libby Hathorn

illustrations by Cassandra Allen

ABC
Books

The ABC 'Wave' device and the 'ABC For Kids' device are trademarks of the Australian Broadcasting Corporation and are used under licence by HarperCollins*Publishers* Australia.

First published in Australia in 2010
by HarperCollins*Publishers* Australia Pty Limited
ABN 36 009 913 517
harpercollins.com.au

HarperCollins*Publishers*
25 Ryde Road, Pymble, Sydney, NSW 2073, Australia
31 View Road, Glenfield, Auckland 0627, New Zealand
A 53, Sector 57, Noida, UP, India
77–85 Fulham Palace Road, London W6 8JB, United Kingdom
2 Bloor Street East, 20th floor, Toronto, Ontario M4W 1A8, Canada
10 East 53rd Street, New York NY 10022, USA

National Library of Australia Cataloguing-in-Publication entry:
The ABC Book of Australian Poetry : a treasury of poems for young people /
    compiled by Libby Hathorn ; illustrator, Cassandra Allen.
     ISBN: 9780733320194 (hbk.)
     Includes index.
     For primary school age.
     Australia — Poetry.
     Hathorn, Libby. Allen, Cassandra.
A821.00803294

Designed and typeset by Jane Waterhouse
Illustrations by Cassandra Allen
Colour reproduction by Graphic Print Group, Adelaide
Printed and bound in China by Phoenix Offset on 128gsm Matt Art

While efforts have been made to trace and acknowledge all copyright holders, in some cases this has been unsuccessful. These copyright holders are very welcome to contact HarperCollins.

5 4 3 2 1   10 11 12 13

A note from Libby Hathorn

My wish for *The ABC Book of Australian Poetry: A Treasury of Poems for Young People* was to compile a rich collection of Australian poetry, peppered with old favourites alongside works of contemporary poets, which would offer readers pleasure and renewed appreciation of our Australian culture and land.

I have been concerned that works of certain classic Australian poets may be slipping out of sight, while the fine works of poets of our time may never be heard or read by young people. This anthology gave me the opportunity to invigorate classic works and highlight contemporary Australian voices, using the metaphor of the river of life for each section, and reflecting so aptly the phases of our history.

I hope that this collection stirs something in the heart and mind of the young and old alike, so that the poems will be shared, read aloud, even sung, for the sheer pleasure of their particular Australian poetic voice and identity.

Part I
All Along the River:
Beginnings

I Am Mary Duroux   20

from **A Song of Rain** C.J. Dennis   21

The Big River Steven Herrick   22

Dilemma Michael Dugan   24

from **Mullumbimby to Bondi Beach**

    J. Andrew Johnstone   25

Part 2
All Along the River:
Mountains, Forests and Plains

Bell-Birds Henry Kendall   30

The Bush James Lister Cuthbertson   33

In the Forest Thomas Shapcott   34

Clinging Mark O'Connor   36

Rainforest Song Libby Hathorn   37

The Bunyips Doug MacLeod   38

The Bunyip Oodgeroo of the Tribe Noonuccal   39

from Bold Jack Donahoe Anonymous   40

Ned Kelly Song Anonymous   42

Said Hanrahan John O'Brien   43

from In Time of Drought Mary Hannay Foott   48

Drought Anonymous   49 *from* **The Never-Never Land** Henry Lawson   50

from **Click Go the Shears** Anonymous   51

Trouble on the Selection Henry Lawson   52

from **The Old Bullock Dray** Anonymous   54

from **Waltzing Matilda** A.B. (Banjo) Paterson   56

The Man from Snowy River A.B. (Banjo) Paterson   58

Parrots Judith Wright   63

Crow-Call Gwen Harwood   64

The Glasshouse Mountains John Foulcher   66

Uluru Eva Johnson   68

In Possum Land Henry Lawson   69

Part 3
All Along the River:
My Country

from **The Law About Singing Out** Gela Nga-Mirraitja   74

My Country Dorothea Mackellar   75

On the Night Train Henry Lawson   78

On Frosty Days David Campbell   79

Nine Miles from Gundagai Jack Moses   80

The Days When We Went Swimming Henry Lawson   82

When the Golden Grain is Ripe J.M. Roache   84

Song of the Rain Hugh McCrae   86

Tanks Rhyll McMaster   87

Rainwater Tank Les A. Murray   88

Old Horses Max Fatchen   90

from **The Old Whim-Horse** Edward Dyson   92

Where the Pelican Builds Her Nest Mary Hannay Foott 94

Frogs Bill Scott 96

The Great Snake Mary Gilmore 97

The Song of the Cicadas Roderic Quinn 98

Tractor William Hart-Smith 100

from The Dusk Robert Gray 101

Ballad of the Drover Henry Lawson 102

Clancy of the Overflow A.B. (Banjo) Patterson 106

Andy's Gone with Cattle Henry Lawson 108

A Tree Kevin Hart 110

Tree Australia Tree Libby Hathorn 112

from Took the Children Away Archie Roach 114

Part 4
All Along the River:
Through the City, Night and Day

Face of the City Grace Perry   120

Supermarket Libby Hathorn   121

The Gardener David Rowbotham   122

Mothers Come Flying Anonymous   123

Profiles of My Father Rhyll McMaster   124

Glenelg Jim Haynes   126

Night Noises Patricia Wrightson   127

Full Moon Robin Klein   128

Nightening Michael Dugan   130

Things That Go Squark Peter Wesley-Smith   131

Sitting on the Fence Michael Leunig   132

Free Wheeling on a Bike Robert Gray   133

The Man from Ironbark A.B. (Banjo) Patterson   134

The Wagtail Judith Wright   137

Peacocks Kate Llewellyn   138

One Return Nicolette Stasko   140

from The Call of the City Victor Daley   142

Part 5
All Along the River: To the Sea

The Beach William Hart-Smith   148

The Sea Lilith Norman   149

Shark Geoffrey Dutton   150

The Sunbather John Thompson   151

Diver R.A. Simpson   152

The Rock Pool Peter Skryznecki   154

Tide Talk Max Fatchen   156

Dolphins Peter McFarlane   158

A Wind from the Sea Randolph Stow   160

Part 6
All Along the River:
Horizon and Beyond

Epiphany Dorothy Hewett   166

Trails Eva Johnson   167

Kingsford-Smith Winifred Tennant   168

Eclipse of the Moon Elizabeth Riddell   169

The Australian Sunrise James Lister Cuthbertson   170

The Star Tribes Fred Biggs   171

No Point in Staying Up Longer David Brooks   172

The People John Tranter   173

Song of the Yellow John Shaw Neilson   174

Be Content Christopher Brennan   176

About Libby Hathorn   179

Sources   180

Index of First Lines   187

Index of Authors and Titles   190

Part I
All Along the River:
Beginnings

I Am

Mary Duroux

I am

the river,

     gently flowing,

     as I wind my way to the sea.

I am

the breeze,

     softly blowing,

     through the leaves of a

     mighty tree.

I am

the snowcapped mountain,

     the frost, the wind, the rains.

I am

a misty fountain,

     the dry and dusty plains.

I am

the sparkle,

     of the early morning dew.

I am

the dream,

     of my mother's dreaming.

Who are you?

From A Song of Rain

C.J. Dennis

Patter, patter ... Boolcoomatta,
Adelaide and Oodnadatta,
Pepegoona, parched and dry,
Laugh beneath a dripping sky.
Riverina's thirsting plain
Knows the benison of rain.
Ararat and Arkaroola
Render thanks with Tantanoola
For the blessings they are gaining,
And it's raining—raining—raining!

Rolls the thunder at Eudunda;
Leongatha, Boort, Kapunda
Send a joyous message down;
Sorrows, flooded, sink and drown.
Ninkerloo and Neerim South
Hail the breaking of the drouth;
From Toolangi's wooded mountains
Sounds the song of splashing fountain
Sovereign summer's might is waning;
And it's raining—raining—raining!

The Big River

Steven Herrick

The big river
rolls past our town
at Hobson's Bend,
takes a slow look
at the houses on stilts
with timber creaking, paint flaking,
at the graveyard hushed
in the lonely shade,
at the fruit bats
dropping mango pulp
into the undergrowth,
at the foundry, and sawmill
grinding under a blazing sun,
at the pub with welcoming verandahs
shaded in wisteria vine,
at Durra Creek surrendering
to the incessant flow,
at Pearce Swamp upstream
on the creek among the willows
and rivergum,

at the storm clouds

rumbling over Rookwood Hill,

at the two boys

casting a line

on the crumbling bank,

at the cow fields

purple with Paterson's curse,

at the jammed tree-trunks

washed down after summer thunder,

at the shop

with dead flies in the window display,

at the mosquito mangroves

and the sucking sound of mud crabs,

at the children throwing mulberries

the stain like lipstick.

The big river

rolls past our town,

takes a slow look,

and rolls away.

Dilemma

Michael Dugan

Coolangatta
Oodnadatta
Wangaratta
What's the matter?
Bindi Bindi
Yarramundi,
I don't know where
to go next Sunday.

From Mullumbimby to Bondi Beach

J. Andrew Johnstone

Mullumbimby, Moree,

Broken Hill and Karalee.

Broke, Yass, Wollondilly.

Oodnadatta, Lilly Pilly.

Maroubra Bay and Parramatta,

Coffin Bay and Coolangatta.

Bronte Cloe'e, Eubalong,

Tamarama and Cooranbong.

Come by Chance and Chukapook

Coogee, Yuna, Mallacoota,

Toorahweenah, Freeman's Reach,

And flamin' perfect Bondi Beach,

Where the tram shoots through

To take you to

Flamin' perfect Bondi Beach!

Adapted from the play *The Tram to Bondi Beach*

Part 2

All Along the River: Mountains, Forests and Plains

Bell-Birds

Henry Kendall

By channels of coolness the echoes are calling,
And down the dim gorges I hear the creek falling:
It lives in the mountain, where moss and the sedges
Touch with their beauty the banks and the ledges.
Through brakes of the cedar and sycamore bowers
Struggles the light that is love to the flowers;
And, softer than slumber, and sweeter than singing,
The notes of the bell-birds are running and ringing.

The silver-voiced bell-birds, the darlings of day-time!
They sing in September their songs of the May-time;
When shadows wax strong, and the thunder-bolts hurtle,
They hide with their fear in the leaves of the myrtle;
When rain and the sunbeams shine mingled together,
They start up like fairies that follow fair weather;
And straightway the hues of their feathers unfolden
Are the green and the purple, the blue and the golden.

October, the maiden of bright yellow tresses,

Loiters for love in these cool wildernesses;

Loiters, knee-deep, in the grasses, to listen,

Where dripping rocks gleam and the leafy pools glisten:

Then is the time when the water-moons splendid

Break with their gold, and are scattered or blended

Over the creeks, till the woodlands have warning

Of songs of the bell-bird and wings of the Morning.

Welcome as waters unkissed by the summers

Are the voices of bell-birds to thirsty far-comers.

When fiery December sets foot in the forest,

And the need of the wayfarer presses the sorest,

Pent in the ridges for ever and ever,

The bell-birds direct him to spring and to river,

With ring and with ripple, like runnels whose torrents

Are toned by the pebbles and leaves in the currents.

Often I sit, looking back to a childhood,

Mixt with the sights and the sounds of the wildwood,

Longing for power and the sweetness to fashion

Lyrics with beats like the heart-beats of Passion;—

Songs interwoven of lights and of laughters

Borrowed from bell-birds in far forest-rafters;

So I might keep in the city and alleys

The beauty and strength of the deep mountain valleys:

Charming to slumber the pain of my losses

With glimpses of creeks and a vision of mosses

The Bush

James Lister Cuthbertson

Give us from dawn to dark
Blue of Australian skies.
Let there be none to mark
Whither our pathway lies.

Give us when noontide comes
Rest in the woodland free—
Fragrant breath of the gums.
Cold, sweet scent of the sea.

Give us the wattle's gold
And the dew-laden air,
And the loveliness bold
Loneliest landscapes wear.

These are the haunts we love,
Glad with enchanted hours.
Bright as the heavens above.
Fresh as the wild bush flowers.

In the Forest

Thomas Shapcott

Wait for the axe sound in the forest.
The birds wait. The lizards pause,
and wait. The creatures that are nearest
earth feel the approaching pace

measure a man. And they must wait.
Then has the time come? The dark
of forest is so solid that
its inter-growth should never break.

But has the time come? The birds
are nervous, see them flinch and turn.
The snake moves into the reeds
quickly. Danger, the signs warn.

That! Slap of an axe. Slap!
There, quick, over there. The tree
is tensed. In its green height
the possums clutch their young; they flee.

Crack again crack of slow man's weapon,
intolerable wait for the one tree's sake
for its grasping fall and its death to happen
and the gash in the forest, and light to break.

Now, says the axe, and the tree is fallen,
the spider crushed in its secret nest.
The late slow lives have been taken,
in the sheltering tree they have been crushed.

The accepted world is quickly broken,
the skull of the forest is opened up.
Now, means the axe. But the birds have forgotten—
there are other trees; they prepare for sleep.

Clinging

Mark O'Connor

To cling, by a breaking fingernail, to an undercut cliff,
not letting your leg pivot and swing out over the valley,
and to note with one eye as you fight off panic,
the faint line of a cycad fossil in that jut of rock
by which your life will hang—this will make your hand
move about the rock, exploring, caressing,
in search of some slight peculiar thing
by which love's fingernail could cling.

Rainforest Song

Libby Hathorn

After a boat trip down the Franklin River in Tasmania

Oh don't bring down
the ancient pine,
the breath of life
that's yours and mine.

Don't tear it out
saw it down,
gouge it, chop it,
let it drown.

Don't fell the tree
that's stood so long,
leave bird and bush
where they belong.

Leave the forest,
green gold place,
the glow of hope
on this earth's
old face.

The Bunyips

Doug MacLeod

At Murray Bridge the bunyips wait
For visitors from interstate
Then up they leap, a sight so strange
And always out of camera range.

The tourists in their mad despair
Start seeing bunyips everywhere
And all the locals join the fun
Saying, 'Bunyips? Pull the other one!'

'What rubbish! Bunyips don't exist!
You must be going round the twist!'
And sure enough, the tourists flee
For fear they've lost their sanity.

While Murray Bridge is all aglow
With cries of 'Thought they'd never go!'
And all along the Murray sands
Are men and bunyips shaking hands.

The Bunyip

Oodgeroo of the Tribe Noonuccal

You keep quiet now, little fella,
You want big-big Bunyip get you?
You look out, no good this place.
You see that waterhole over there?
He Gooborra, Silent Pool.
Suppose it you go close up one time
Big fella woor, he wait there,
Big fella Bunyip sit down there,
In Silent Pool many bones down there.
He come up when it is dark,
He belong the big dark, that one.
Don't go away from camp fire, you,
Better you curl up in the gunya.
Go to sleep now, little fella,
Tonight he hungry, hear him roar,
He frighten us, the terrible woor,
He the secret thing, he Fear,
He something we don't know.
Go to sleep now, little fella.
Curl up with the yella dingo.

From Bold Jack Donahoe

Anonymous

'Twas of a valiant highwayman and outlaw of disdain
Who'd scorn to live in slavery or wear a convict's chain;
His name it was Jack Donahoe of courage and renoun—
He'd scorn to live in slavery or humble to the Crown.

This bold, undaunted highwayman, as you may understand,
Was banished for his natural life from Erin's happy land.
In Dublin city of renoun, where his first breath he drew,
It's there they titled him the brave and bold Jack Donahoe.

He scarce had been a twelvemonth on the Australian shore,
When he took to the highway, as oft he had before,
Brave MacNamara, Underwood, Webber and Walmsley too,
These were the four associates of bold Jack Donahoe.

As Jack and his companions roved out one afternoon,
Not thinking that the pains of death would overcome so soon,
To their surprise five horse police appeared all in their view,
And in quick time they did advance to take Jack Donahoe.

'Come, come, you cowardly rascals, oh, do not run away!
We'll fight them man to man, my boys, their number's only three;
For I'd rather range the bush around, like dingo or kangaroo,
Than work one hour for Government,' said bold Jack Donahoe.

'Oh, no,' said cowardly Walmsley, 'to that I won't agree;
I see they're still advancing us—their number's more than three.
And if we wait we'll be too late, the battle we will rue.'
'Then begone from me, you cowardly dog,' replied Jack Donahoe.

The Sergeant of the horse police discharged his car-a-bine,
And called aloud to Donahoe, 'Will you fight or resign?'
'Resign, no, no! I never will, until your cowardly crew,
For today I'll fight with all my might,' cried bold Jack Donahoe.

The Sergeant then, in a hurry his party to divide,
Placed one to fire in front of him, and another on each side;
The Sergeant and the Corporal, they both fired too,
Till the fatal ball had pierced the heart of bold Jack Donahoe.

Six rounds he fought those horse police before the fatal ball,
Which pierced his heart with cruel smart, caused Donahoe to fall;
And as he closed his mournful eyes he bade this world adieu,
Saying, 'Good people all, pray for the soul of poor Jack Donahoe.'

Ned Kelly Song

Anonymous

Ned Kelly was born in a ramshackle hut,
He'd battled since he was a kid:
He grew up with bad men and duffers and thieves,
And learnt all the bad things they did.

Now down at Glenrowan they held up the pub,
And were having a drink and a song,
When the troopers rolled up and surrounded the place;
The Kellys had waited too long.

Some say he's a hero and gave to the poor,
While others, 'A killer,' they say;
But to me it just proves the old saying is true,
The saying that crime doesn't pay.

Yet, when I look round at some people I know,
And the prices of things that we buy;
I just think to myself, well perhaps, after all,
Old Ned wasn't such a bad guy.

Said Hanrahan

John O'Brien

'We'll all be rooned,' said Hanrahan,
In accents most forlorn,
Outside the church, ere Mass began,
One frosty Sunday morn.

The congregation stood about,
Coat-collars to the ears,
And talked of stock, and crops, and drought,
As it had done for years.

'It's lookin' crook,' said Daniel Croke;
'Bedad, it's cruke, me lad,
For never since the banks went broke
Has seasons been so bad.'

'It's dry, all right,' said young O'Neil,
With which astute remark
He squatted down upon his heel
And chewed a piece of bark.

And so around the chorus ran
'It's keepin' dry, no doubt.'
'We'll all be rooned,' said Hanrahan,
'Before the year is out.

'The crops are done; ye'll have your work
To save one bag of grain;
From here way out to Back-o'-Bourke
They're singin' out for rain.

'They're singin' out for rain,' he said,
'And all the tanks are dry.'
The congregation scratched its head,
And gazed around the sky.

'There won't be grass, in any case,
Enough to feed an ass;
There's not a blade on Casey's place
As I came down to Mass.'

'If rain don't come this month,' said Dan,
And cleared his throat to speak—
'We'll all be rooned,' said Hanrahan,
'If rain don't come this week.'

A heavy silence seemed to steal
On all at this remark;
And each man squatted on his heel,
And chewed a piece of bark.

'We want an inch of rain, we do,'
O'Neil observed at last;
But Croke 'maintained' we wanted two
To put the danger past.

'If we don't get three inches, man,
Or four to break this drought,
We'll all he rooned,' said Hanrahan,
'Before the year is out.'

In God's good time down came the rain;
And all the afternoon
On iron roof and window-pane
It drummed a homely tune.

And through the night it pattered still,
And lightsome, gladsome elves
On dripping spout and window-sill
Kept talking to themselves.

It peleted, pelted all day long,
A-singing at its work,
Till every heart took up the song
Way out to Back-o'-Bourke.

And every creek a banker ran,
And dams filled overtop;
'We'll all he rooned,' said Hanrahan,
'If this rain doesn't stop.'

And stop it did, in God's good time;
And spring came in to fold
A mantle o'er the hills sublime
Of green and pink and gold.

And days went by on dancing feet,
With harvest-hopes immense,
And laughing eyes beheld the wheat
Nid-nodding o'er the fence.

And, oh, the smiles on every face,
As happy lad and lass
Through grass knee-deep on Casey's place
Went riding down to Mass.

While round the church in clothes genteel
Discoursed the men of mark,
And each man squatted on his heel,
And chewed a piece of bark.

'There'll be bush-fires for sure, me man,
There will, without a doubt;
We'll all be rooned,' said Hanrahan,
'Before the year is out.'

From In Time of Drought

Mary Hannay Foott

The river of God is full of water—Psalm

The rushes are black by the river bed,
And the sheep and the cattle stand
Wistful-eyed—where the waters were—
In a waste of gravel and sand;
Or pass o'er their dying and dead to slake
Their thirst at the slimy pool.
Shall they pine and perish in pangs of drought,
While Thy river, 0 God, is full!

The fields are furrowed, the seed is sown,
But no dews from the heavens are shed;
And where shall the grain for the harvest be—?
And how shall the poor be fed?
In waterless gullies they winnow the earth,
New-turned by the miner's tool;
And the wayfarer faints 'neath his lightened load—
Yet the river of God is full.

Drought

Anonymous

Wearily watching and waiting for rain,
Looking to heaven, and looking in vain,
Crying in anguish, again and again,
   How long, O Lord!
Drought-stricken plains stretching lifeless and bare,
Drought-stricken river beds parched and dry,
Drought-stricken carcasses tainting the air,
Nature despairing re-echoes the cry,
   How long, O Lord!

From The Never-Never Land

Henry Lawson

By hut, homestead, and shearing-shed,
By railroad, coach, and track—
By lonely graves where rest our dead,
Up-Country and Out-Back:
To where beneath the clustered stars
The dreamy plains expand—
My home lies wide a thousand miles
In the Never-Never Land.

It lies beyond the farming belt,
Wide wastes of scrub and plain,
A blazing desert in the drought,
A wake-land after rain;
To the skyline sweeps the waving grass,
Or whirls the scorching sand—
A phantom land, a mystic realm!
The Never-Never Land.

From Click Go the Shears

Anonymous

Out on the board the old shearer stands,
Grasping his shears in his long, bony hands,
Fixed is his gaze on a bare-bellied 'joe',
Glory if he gets her, won't he make the ringer go.

Chorus
Click go the shears boys, click, click, click,
Wide is his blow and his hands move quick,
The ringer looks around and is beaten by a blow,
And curses the old snagger with the blue-bellied 'joe'.

In the middle of the floor in his cane-bottomed chair
Is the boss of the board, with eyes everywhere;
Notes well each fleece as it comes to the screen,
Paying strict attention if it's taken off clean.

Chorus
Click go the shears boys, click, click, click,
Wide is his blow and his hands move quick,
The ringer looks around and is beaten by a blow,
And curses the old snagger with the blue-bellied 'joe'.

Trouble on the Selection

Henry Lawson

You lazy boy, you're here at last,
You must be wooden-legged;
Now, are you sure the gate is fast
And all the sliprails pegged,
And all the milkers at the yard,
The calves all in the pen?
We don't want Poley's calf to suck
His mother dry again.

And did you mend the broken rail
And make it firm and neat?
I s'pose you want that brindle steer
All night among the wheat.
And if he finds the lucerne patch,
He'll stuff his belly full;
He'll eat till he gets 'blown' on that
And busts like Ryan's bull.

Old Spot is lost? You'll drive me mad,
You will, upon my soul!
She might be in the boggy swamps
Or down a digger's hole.
You needn't talk, you never looked;
You'd find her if you'd choose,
Instead of poking 'possum logs
And hunting kangaroos.

How came your boots as wet as muck?
You tried to drown the ants!
Why don't you take your bluchers off?
Good Lord, he's tore his pants!
Your father's coming home to-night;
You'll catch it hot, you'll see.
Now go and wash your filthy face
And come and get your tea.

From The Old Bullock Dray

Anonymous

Now the shearing is all over, and the wool is coming down
I mean to get a wife, my boys, when I go down to town
For everything has got a mate that brings itself to view
From the little paddy-melon to the big kangaroo

Chorus
So roll up your blankets and let us make a push
I'll take you up the country and show you the bush
I'll be bound such a chance you won't get another day
So roll up and take possession of the old bullock dray

I'll teach you the whip and the bullocks how to flog
You'll be my off-sider when we're fast in the bog
Hitting out both left and right and every other way
Making skin and blood and hair fly round the old bullock dray

Good beef and damper, of that you'll get enough
When boiling in the bucket such a walloper of duff
Our mates, they'll all dance and sing upon our wedding day
To the music of the bells around the old bullock dray

Now that we are married and have children five times three
No one lives so happy as my little wife and me
She goes out a-hunting to while away the day
While I take down the wool upon the old bullock dray.

A paddy-melon is a small and speedy marsupial.

From Waltzing Matilda

A.B. (Banjo) Paterson

Oh there once was a swagman camped in the billabongs,
Under the shade of a Coolibah tree;
And he sang as he looked at his old billy boiling,
'Who'll come a-waltzing Matilda with me?'

Chorus
Who'll come a-waltzing Matilda, my darling.
Who'll come a-waltzing Matilda with me?
Waltzing Matilda and leading a water-bag,
Who'll come a-waltzing Matilda with me?

Up came the jumbuck to drink at the waterhole,
Up jumped the swagman and grabbed him in glee;
And he sang as he put him away in his tucker-bag,
'You'll come a-waltzing Matilda with me.'

Up came the squatter a-riding his thoroughbred;
Up came policemen—one, two, and three.
'Whose is the jumbuck you've got in the tucker-bag?
You'll come a-waltzing Matilda with we.'

Up sprang the swagman, and he jumped in the waterhole,
Drowning himself by the Coolibah tree;
And his voice can be heard as it sings in the billabongs,
'Who'll come a-waltzing Matilda with me.'

The Man from Snowy River

A.B. (Banjo) Paterson

There was movement at the station, for the word had passed around
That the colt from old Regret had got away,
And had joined the wild bush horses—he was worth a thousand pound,
So all the cracks had gathered to the fray.
All the tried and noted riders from the stations near and far
Had mustered at the homestead overnight,
For the bushmen love hard riding where the wild bush horses are,
And the stockhorse snuffs the battle with delight.

There was Harrison, who made his pile when Pardon won the cup,
The old man with his hair as white as snow;
But few could ride beside him when his blood was fairly up—
He would go wherever horse and man could go.
And Clancy of the Overflow came down to lend a hand,
No better horseman ever held the reins;
For never horse could throw him while the saddle girths would stand,
He learnt to ride while droving on the plains.

And one was there, a stripling on a small and weedy beast,
He was something like a racehorse undersized,
With a touch of Timor pony—three parts thoroughbred at least—
And such as are by mountain horsemen prized.
He was hard and tough and wiry—just the sort that won't say die—
There was courage in his quick impatient tread;
And he bore the badge of gameness in his bright and fiery eye,
And the proud and lofty carriage of his head.

But still so slight and weedy, one would doubt his power to stay,
And the old man said, 'That horse will never do
For a long and tiring gallop—lad, you'd better stop away,
Those hills are far too rough for such as you.'
So he waited sad and wistful—only Clancy stood his friend—
'I think we ought to let him come,' he said;
'I warrant he'll be with us when he's wanted at the end,
For both his horse and he are mountain bred.

'He hails from Snowy River, up by Kosciusko's side,
Where the hills are twice as steep and twice as rough,
Where a horse's hoofs strike firelight from the flint stones every stride,
The man that holds his own is good enough.
And the Snowy River riders on the mountains make their home,
Where the river runs those giant hills between;
I have seen full many horsemen since I first commenced to roam,
But nowhere yet such horsemen have I seen.'

So he went—they found the horses by the big mimosa clump—
They raced away towards the mountain's brow,
And the old man gave his orders, 'Boys, go at them from the jump,
No use to try for fancy riding now.
And, Clancy, you must wheel them, try and wheel them to the right.
Ride boldly, lad, and never fear the spills,
For never yet was rider that could keep the mob in sight,
If once they gain the shelter of those hills.'

So Clancy rode to wheel them—he was racing on the wing
Where the best and boldest riders take their place,
And he raced his stockhorse past them, and he made the ranges ring
With the stockwhip, as he met them face to face.
Then they halted for a moment, while he swung the dreaded lash,
But they saw their well-loved mountain full in view,
And they charged beneath the stockwhip with a sharp and sudden dash,
And off into the mountain scrub they flew.

Then fast the horsemen followed, where the gorges deep and black
Resounded to the thunder of their tread,
And the stockwhip woke the echoes, and they fiercely answered back
From cliffs and crags that beetled overhead.
And upward, ever upward, the wild horses held their way,
Where mountain ash and kurrajong grew wide;
And the old man muttered fiercely, 'We may bid the mob good day,
No man can hold them down the other side.'

When they reached the mountain's summit, even Clancy took a pull,

It well might make the boldest hold their breath,

The wild hop scrub grew thickly, and the hidden ground was full

Of wombat holes, and any slip was death.

But the man from Snowy River let the pony have his head,

And he swung his stockwhip round and gave a cheer,

And he raced him down the mountain like a torrent down its bed,

While the others stood and watched in very fear.

He sent the flint stones flying, but the pony kept his feet,

He cleared the fallen timber in his stride,

And the man from Snowy River never shifted in his seat—

It was grand to see that mountain horseman ride.

Through the stringybarks and saplings, on the rough and broken ground,

Down the hillside at a racing pace he went;

And he never drew the bridle till he landed safe and sound,

At the bottom of that terrible descent.

He was right among the horses as they climbed the further hill,

And the watchers on the mountain, standing mute,

Saw him ply the stockwhip fiercely, he was right among them still,

As he raced across the clearing in pursuit.

Then they lost him for a moment, where two mountain gullies met

In the ranges, but a final glimpse reveals

On a dim and distant hillside the wild horses racing yet,

With the man from Snowy River at their heels.

And he ran them single-handed till their sides were white with foam.

He followed like a bloodhound on their track,

Till they halted, cowed and beaten, then he turned their heads for home,

And alone and unassisted brought them back.

But his hardy mountain pony he could scarcely raise a trot,

He was blood from hip to shoulder from the spur;

But his pluck was still undaunted, and his courage fiery hot,

For never yet was mountain horse a cur.

And down by Kosciusko, where the pine-clad ridges raise

Their torn and rugged battlements on high,

Where the air is clear as crystal, and the white stars fairly blaze

At midnight in the cold and frosty sky,

And where around The Overflow the reed beds sweep and sway

To the breezes, and the rolling plains are wide,

The man from Snowy River is a household word today,

And the stockmen tell the story of his ride.

Parrots

Judith Wright

Loquats are cold as winter suns.
Among rough leaves their clusters glow
like oval beads of cloudy amber,
or small fat flames of birthday candles.

Parrots, when the winter dwindles
their forest fruits and seeds, remember
where the swelling loquats grow,
how chill and sweet their thin juice runs,

and shivering in the morning cold
we draw the curtains back and see
the lovely greed of their descending,
the lilt of flight that blurs their glories,

and warm our eyes upon the lories
and the rainbow-parrots landing.
There's not a fruit on any tree
to match their crimson, green and gold.

To see them cling and sip and sway,
loquats are no great price to pay.

Crow-Call

Gwen Harwood

'He lives eternally who lives in the present' Tractatus 6.4311

Let this be eternal life:
light ebbing, my dinghy drifting
on watershine, dead centre
of cloud and cloud-reflection—
high vapour, mind's illusion.

And for music, Baron Corvo,
my half tame forest raven
with his bad leg unretracted
beating for home, lamenting
or, possibly, rejoicing
that he saw the world at all.

Space of a crow-call, enclosing
the self and all it remembers.
Heart-beat, wing-beat, a moment.
My line jerks taut. The cod
are biting. This too is eternal;
the death of cod at twilight.
And this: food on my table
keeping a tang of the ocean.

So many, in raven darkness.
Why give death fancy names?

Corvo, where have you settled
your crippled leg for the night?

The Glasshouse Mountains

John Foulcher

The freeway
is riddled with cars.
At every exit, the new estates
cluster among ruins
of rainforest:
houses spread like fungus
down the thick grey trunks
of streets, fallen
everywhere. Video shops.
Clubs. Supermarkets,
white-anted
with trolleys. A golf course
gashes the hill's flank.
The pineapple plantations,
sharp and brittle—how
they seem to itch
in the furrowed dirt.

And above, worn away
from an older crust,
the Glasshouse Mountains leap
across the dying plain,
the sun carving shadows
from their tall storeys;
they lift like voices,
their hard volcanic echoes
heard faintly, all along the coast.

Uluru

Eva Johnson

Isolated rock,
   that stands in silence
caress the earth,
   while waters of tears
carry ancient stories
down your jagged crevasses,
   to crystal pools
where women sing, wash, dance,
   in ritual, protect
the secrets of your dreaming.
Hear their voices, their wails,
   that echo against your ochred walls
whilst you stand dormant
   only to be awakened
by voices of your keepers.

In Possum Land

Henry Lawson

In Possum Land the nights are fair,
The streams are fresh and clear;
No dust is in the moonlit air,
No traffic jars the ear.

With possums gambolling overhead,
'Neath western stars so grand,
Ah! would that we could make our bed,
To-night in Possum Land.

Part 3

All Along the River: My Country

From The Law About Singing Out

Gela Nga-Mirraitja

My father used to do it. We used to get up early in the morning and he'd sing out and talk. Sometimes he didn't talk early in the morning, only when travelling and we used to stop and he'd talk then in language.

It would make you look carefully at the country, so you could see the signs, so you could see which way to go . . .

The law about singing out was made like that to make you notice that all the trees here are your countrymen, your relations. All the trees and the birds are your relations.

There are different kinds of birds here. They can't talk to you straight up. You've got to sing out to them so that they can know you . . .

That's why I talked to the birds this morning, and all the birds were happy. All the birds were really happy and sang out: 'Oh! That's a relation of ours. That's a relation we didn't know about.' That's the way they spoke, and they were happy then to sing out.

My Country

Dorothea Mackellar

The love of field and coppice
Of green and shaded lanes
Of ordered woods and gardens
Is running in your veins—
Strong love of grey-blue distance,
Brown streams and soft, dim skies…
I know but cannot share it,
My love is otherwise.

I love a sunburnt country,
A land of sweeping plains
Of ragged mountain ranges
Of droughts and flooding rains.
I love her far horizons
I love her jewel-sea,
Her beauty and her terror—
The wide brown land for me!

The stark white ringbarked forests
All tragic 'neath the moon
The sapphire-misted mountains
The hot gold hush of noon—
Green tangle of the brushes
Where lithe lianas coil
And orchid-laden tree-ferns
Smother the cimson soil.

Core of my heart, my country—
Her pitiless blue sky,
When sick at heart around us
We see the cattle die…
But then the grey clouds gather
And we can bless again,
The drumming of an army,
The steady, soaking rain.

Core of my heart, my country,
Land of the Rainbow Gold—
For flood and fire and famine
She pays us back three-fold…
Over the thirsty paddocks,
Watch, after many days,
The filmy veil of greenness
That thickens as we gaze…

An opal-hearted country,
A wilful, lavish land—
Ah, you who have not loved her,
You will not understand…
The world is fair and splendid…
But whensoe'er I die
I know to what brown country
My homing thoughts will fly!

On the Night Train

Henry Lawson

Have you seen the Bush by moonlight, from the train, go running by?
Blackened log and stump and sapling, ghostly trees all dead and dry;
Here a patch of glassy water; there a glimpse of mystic sky?
Have you heard the still voice calling – yet so warm, and yet so cold:
'I'm the Mother-Bush that bore you! Come to me when you are old'?

Did you see the Bush below you sweeping darkly to the Range,
All unchanged and all unchanging, yet so very old and strange!
While you thought in softened anger of the things that did estrange?
(Did you hear the Bush a-calling, when your heart was young and bold:
'I'm the Mother-Bush that nursed you; come to me when you are old'?)

In the cutting or the tunnel, out of sight of stock or shed,
Have you heard the grey Bush calling from the pine-ridge overhead:
'You have seen the seas and cities – all is cold to you, or dead –
All seems done and all seems told, but the grey-light turns to gold!
I'm the Mother-Bush that loves you – come to me now you are old'?

On Frosty Days

David Campbell

On frosty days, when I was young,
I rode out early with the men
And mustered cattle till their long
Blue shadows covered half the plain;

And when we turned our horses round,
Only the homestead's point of light,
Men's voices, and the bridles' sound,
Were left in the enormous night.

And now again the sun has set
All yellow and a greening sky
Sucks up the colour from the wheat—
And here's my horse, my dog and I.

Nine Miles from Gundagai

Jack Moses

I've done my share of shearing sheep,
Of droving and all that,
And bogged a bullock-team as well
On a Murrumbidgee flat.
I've seen the bullock stretch and strain,
And blink his bleary eye,
And the dog sit on the tucker box
Nine miles from Gundagai.

I've been jilted, jarred, and crossed in love,
And sand-bagged in the dark,
Till if a mountain fell on me
I'd treat it as a lark.
It's when you've got your bullocks bogged,
That's the time you flog and cry,
And the dog sits on the tucker box,
Nine miles from Gundagai.

We've all got our little troubles,

In life's hard, thorny way.

Some strike them in a motor car

And others in a dray.

But when your dog and bullocks strike,

It ain't no apple pie,

And the dog sat on the tucker box

Nine miles from Gundagai.

But that's all past and dead and gone,

And I've sold the team for meat,

And perhaps some day where I was bogged,

There'll be an asphalt street.

The dog, ah! well he got a bait,

And thought he'd like to die,

So I buried him in the tucker box,

Nine miles from Gundagai.

The Days When We Went Swimming

Henry Lawson

The breezes waved the silver grass,
Waist-high along the siding,
And to the creek we ne'er could pass
Three boys on bare-back riding;
Beneath the sheoaks in the bend
The waterhole was brimming –
Do you remember yet, old friend,
The times we 'went in swimming'?

The days we 'played the wag' from school –
Joys shared – and paid for singly –
The air was hot, the water cool –
And naked boys are kingly!
With mud for soap the sun to dry –
A well planned lie to stay us,
And dust well rubbed on neck and face
Lest cleanliness betray us.

And you'll remember farmer Kutz –
Though scarcely for his bounty –
He leased a forty-acre block,
And thought he owned the county;
A farmer of the old world school,
That men grew hard and grim in,
He drew his water from the pool
That we preferred to swim in.

And do you mind when down the creek
His angry way he wended,
A green-hide cartwhip in his hand
For our young backs intended?
Three naked boys upon the sand –
Half buried and half sunning –
Three startled boys without their clothes
Across the paddocks running.

We've had some scares, but we looked blank
When resting there and chumming,
One glance by chance along the bank
And saw the farmer coming!
And home impressions linger yet
Of cups of sorrow brimming;
I hardly think that we'll forget
The last day we went swimming.

When the Golden Grain is Ripe

J.M. Roache

Written during the changeover from horse-drawn ploughs and headers to tractors.

I will see you in November
When the days are long and bright,
I'll meet you at the harvest
When the golden grain is ripe.
I am looking to the future
Of bumper crops to come
When I'm sitting on the tractor
Beneath the blazing sun.

With dust clouds slowly rising
From beneath the header frame,
I'll hear the old drum roaring
As it's belting out the grain.
Bags of wheat upon the lorries
We'll be sending to the train
And all our cares and worries
Will soon be gone again.

I am longing for the summer
When the harvest moons are bright,
And I'll leave so far behind me
These dazzling city lights.
So I'll see you in November
When the days are long and light,
And I'll meet you at the harvest
When the golden grain is ripe.

Song of the Rain

Hugh McCrae

Night,
And the yellow pleasure of candle-light …
Old brown books and the kind fine face of the clock
Fogged in the veils of the fire—its cuddling tock.

The cat,
Greening her eyes on the flame-litten mat;
Wickedly wakeful she yawns at the rain
Bending the roses over the pane,
And a bird in my heart begins to sing
Over and over the same sweet thing—

Safe in the house with my boyhood's love
And our children asleep in the attic above.

Tanks

Rhyll McMaster

Travelling,
where darkness hauls the world
back underground,
we pass a solid water tank;
squatting on wooden stumps
its corrugations gleam the dull combusting silver
of elephant hide.

Summer nights breed tanks
and a belief that the moon
was made from a tank smashed into sky passage,
empty and dank, corroded by lichens.

In hollows behind outhouses
or back of a wall of pepper trees, tanks
are sleeping, stirring.
They expand, become nervous and rough
and, grinning with iron dimples,
begin to move out to the edge of town
to wait for the lorry to Places Unknown.

Rainwater Tank

Les A. Murray

Empty rings when tapped give tongue,
rings that are tense with water talk:
as he sounds them ring by rung,
Joe Mitchell's reddened knuckles walk.

The cattledog's head sinks down a notch
and another notch, beside the tank,
and Mitchell's boy, with an old jack-plane,
lifts moustaches from a plank.

From the puddle that the tank has dripped
hens peck glimmerings and uptilt
their heads to shape the quickness down;
petunias live on what gets spilt.

The tankstand spider adds a spittle
thread to her portrait of her soul.
Pencil-grey and stacked like shillings
out of a banker's paper roll

stands the tank, roof-water drinker.
The downpipe stares drought into it.
Briefly the kitchen tap turns on
then off. But the tank says Debit, Debit.

From The Old Whim-Horse

Edward Dyson

He's an old grey horse, with his head bowed sadly,
And with dim old eyes and a queer roll aft,
With the off-fore sprung and the hind screwed badly
And he bears all over the brands of graft;
And he lifts his head from the grass to wonder
Why by night and day now the whim is still,
Why the silence is, and the stampers' thunder
Sounds forth no more from the shattered mill.

In that whim he worked when the night winds bellowed
On the riven summit of Giant's Hand,
And by day when prodigal Spring had yellowed
All the wide, long sweep of enchanted land;
And he knew his shift, and the whistle's warning,
And he knew the calls of the boys below;
Through the years, unbidden, at night or morning,
He had taken his stand by the old whim bow.

But the whim stands still, and the wheeling swallow
In the silent shaft hangs her home of clay,
And the lizards flirt and the swift snakes follow
O'er the grass-grown brace in the summer day;
And the corn springs high in the cracks and corners
Of the forge, and down where the timber lies;
And the crows are perched like a band of mourners
On the broken hut on the Hermit's Rise.

A whim is a vertical drum driven by horse power.

Frogs

Bill Scott

Fat frogs squat greenly
in waterholes.
Swim with hind legs
on hinges.

They sleep all day
under tank-stands
where damp fern fronds
hang in fringes.

But on blowy nights
when rain rattles
on the stiff leaves
of palm and mango,

they swell their throats,
bellow, honk and tinkle—
that's what I call
a frog fandango.

The Great Snake

Mary Gilmore

Into a hole into the ground he went,
Into a hole and the darkness before him;
Into the hole he went, and the dark
About him; into the hole he went
And the dark behind him.

No light of moon or sun
Was with him there;
Then with a rock earth closed him in.

Forever he sleeps, save that
Sometimes in dreams he turns.
Then the mountains are shaken,

The Song of the Cicadas

Roderic Quinn

Yesterday there came to me
From a green and graceful tree,
As I loitered listlessly
Nothing doing, nothing caring,
Light and warmth and fragrance sharing
With the butterfly and bee,
While the sapling-tops a-glisten
Danced and trembled, wild and willing,
Such a sudden sylvan shrilling
That I could not choose but listen.

Green cicadas, black cicadas,
Happy in the gracious weather,
Floury-baker, double-drummer,
All as one and all together,
How they voiced the golden summer!

Stealing back there came to me
As I loitered listlessly
'Neath the green and graceful tree,
Nothing doing, nothing caring,

Boyhood moments spent in sharing
With the butterfly and bee
Youth and freedom, warmth and glamour,
While cicadas round me shrilling,
Set the sleepy noontide thrilling
With their keen insistent clamour.

Green cicadas, black cicadas,
Happy in the gracious weather,
Floury-bakers, double-drummers
All as one and all together—
How they voiced the bygone summers!

Tractor

William Hart-Smith

Dragging an iron rake
the tractor wallows
across the ocean of the paddock
with a fine excitement of gulls
in its wake.

It has two large paddle wheels,
a funnel, with smoke;
and the captain is on the bridge.
Having cast off a couple
of moments ago,
he sets a course for the opposite hedge.

From The Dusk

Robert Gray

A kangaroo is standing up, and dwindling like a plant
with a single bud.
Fur combed into a line
in the middle of its chest,
a bow-wave
under slanted light, out in the harbour.

And its fine unlined face is held on the cool air;
a face in which you feel
the small thrust-forward teeth lying in the lower jaw,
grass-stained and sharp.

Standing beyond a wire fence, in weeds,
against the bush that is like a wandering smoke.

Mushroom-coloured,
and its white chest, the underside of a growing mushroom,
in the last daylight.

Ballad of the Drover

Henry Lawson

Across the stony ridges,
Across the rolling plain,
Young Harry dale, the drover,
Comes riding home again.
And well his stock-horse bears him,
And light of heart is he,
And stoutly his old packhorse
Is trotting by his knee.

Up Queensland way with cattle
He's travelled regions vast;
And many months have vanished
Since home-folks saw him last.
He hums a song of someone
He hopes to marry soon;
And hobble-chains and camp-ware
Keep jingling to the tune.

Beyond the hazy dado
Against the lower skies
And yon blue line of ranges
The station homestead lies.
And thitherward the drover
Jogs through the lazy noon,
While hobble-chains and camp-ware
Are jingling to a tune

An hour has filled the heavens
With storm-clouds inky black;
At times the lightning trickles
Around the drover's track;
But Harry pushed onward,
His horses' strength he tries,
In hope to reach the river
Before the flood shall rise.

The thunder, pealing o'er him,
Goes rumbling down the plain;
And sweet on thirsty pastures
Beats fast the plashing rain;
The every creek and gully
Sends forth its tribute flood—
The river runs a banker,
All stained with yellow mud.

Clancy of the Overflow

A.B. (Banjo) Paterson

I had written him a letter which I had, for want of better
Knowledge, sent to where I met him down the Lachlan years ago;
He was shearing when I knew him, so I sent the letter to him.
Just 'on spec', addressed as follows, 'Clancy, of The Overflow.'

And an answer came directed in a writing unexpected,
(And I think the same was written with a thumb-nail dipped in tar)
'Twas his shearing mate who wrote it, and verbatim I will quote it:
'Clancy's gone to Queensland droving, and we don't know where he are.'

In my wild erratic fancy visions come to me of Clancy
Gone a-droving 'down the Cooper' where the Western drovers go;
As the stock are slowly stringing, Clancy rides behind them singing,
For the drover's life has pleasures that the townsfolk never know.

And the bush has friends to meet him, and their kindly voices greet him
In the murmur of the breezes and the river on its bars,
And he sees the vision splendid of the sunlit plains extended,
And at night the wond'rous glory or the everlasting stars.

I am sitting in my dingy little office, where a stingy
Ray of sunlight struggles feebly down between the houses tall,
And the foetid air and gritty of the dusty, dirty city,
Through the open window floating, spreads its foulness over all

And in place of lowing cattle, I can hear the fiendish rattle
Of the tramways and the 'buses making hurry down the street;
And the language uninviting of the gutter children fighting,
Comes fitfully and faintly through the ceaseless tramp of feet.

And the hurrying people daunt me, and their pallid faces haunt me
As they shoulder one another in their rush and nervous haste,
With their eager eyes and greedy, and their stunted forms and weedy,
For townsfolk have no time to grow, they have no time to waste.

And I somehow rather fancy that I'd like to change with Clancy,
Like to take a turn at droving where the seasons come and go,
While he faced the round eternal of the cash-book and the journal—
But I doubt he'd suit the office, Clancy, of 'The Overflow'.

Andy's Gone with Cattle

Henry Lawson

Our Andy's gone with cattle now—
Our hearts are out of order—
With drought he's gone to battle now
Across the Queensland border.

He's left us in dejection now,
Our thoughts with him are roving;
It's dull on this selection now,
Since Andy went a-droving.

Who now shall wear the cheerful face
In times when things are slackest?
And who shall whistle round the place
When Fortune frowns her blackest?

Oh, who shall cheek the squatter now
When he comes round us snarling?
His tongue is growing hotter now
Since Andy crossed the Darling.

Oh, may the showers in torrents fall,
And all the tanks run over;
And may the grass grow green and tall
In pathways of the drover;

And may good angels send the rain
On desert stretches sandy;
And when the summer comes again
God grant 'twill bring us Andy.

A Tree

Kevin Hart

It takes a life to understand a tree.
You start by climbing high, by holding eggs
Like eyes in the curved eyelids of a young hand,
Then take away plump scratchy nests, still warm,

By thinking other things. Branches will wave
As though to seek your help, but then they go
Just like the ants and leaves marked hard with lines.
Summer will pass with rich dark smells of earth

And then the sound of wind in branches—yes,
That too will slide into the void you hold
With next door's silky oak that vaguely sighed
One early morning, deep in the pulp of Spring,

Then fell on power lines and through a house.
It takes a life to understand a tree
But life climbs quickly, climbs with claws, and so
You haven't stood beneath a tree for long

And all that's left is a sparkle up there, high,
A glistening that you can hardly see,
That beckons you toward it, nonetheless,
And somehow tells you that there is no void.

Tree Australia Tree

Libby Hathorn

Hey, bottlebrush you!

When your fire-flowers enchant us,

I know why the bush birds

Are drawn to your branches.

And banksia gnarled,

So strange by the moon,

Who could not wonder

At your woody blooms?

Tree Australia Tree

Hey, rainforest monarch!

With your buttress so grand,

Who could walk in your forests

And not understand?

Boxwood, strangler fig,

Stinging tree, cedar rare.

All have their own place,

All belong here.

Tree Australia Tree

Hey, boab so fat!
With your water in store,
Only they share your secret
Who know the bush lore.
Hey, scribbly gum, river gum,
Ghost gum supreme!
If eucalypt's king here
Then wattle is queen.

For you, sumptuous wattle,
Ablaze, yellow bold,
Who cannot delight
In your great gusts of gold?

Tree Australia Tree
Tree Australia Tree
Tree Australia Tree

From Took the Children Away

Archie Roach

This story's right, the story's true
I would not tell lies to you
Like the promises they did not keep
And how they fenced us in like sheep
Said to us come take our hand
Sent us off to mission land
Taught us to read, to write and pray,
Then took the children away.
Took the Children away
The Children away
Snatched from their mother's breast
Said it was for the best
Took them away…

One sweet day all the children came back

The children came back

The children came back

Back where their hearts grow strong

Back where they all belong

The children came back

Said the children came back

The children came back

Back where they understand

Back to their mother's land

The children came back.

Back to their mother

Back to their father

Back to their sister

Back to their brother

Back to their people

Back to their land

All the children come back

The children come back

The children come back

Yes I came back.

Part 4

All Along the River: Through the City, Night and Day

Face of the City

Grace Perry

They are changing the face of the city;
old buildings of sandstone are tumbling down.
The drill bites deep till raw nerves tremble,
and steel on steel scream shatters ground.
Unanaesthetised but uncomplaining,
cavernous mouth and haunted eyes
feel each shiver of wide incisions,
retracted muscles quivering
as rough hands chisel at splintered bone,
and a whistle shrills for the man suspended
above the ruin and broken stones.

Supermarket

Libby Hathorn

There's the jingle and the jangle
Of the trolleys when they tangle,
Toilet tissue, cracker biscuits, what to choose?
Canned tomatoes, and lime jelly
Nuts and raisins, vermicelli
Rice and flour, pickles sour as we cruise.

There's the whooshing and the wheezing
Of the doors where food is freezing—
Choc chip icecream, frozen vegies
Stacks of packets brightly teasing.

There's the humming and the ha-ing,
Dark green apples or bright red?
Runny honey or the candied?
Crusty buns or fresh sliced bread?

There's the wiling and the waiting
In the checkout queue and then
There's the adding, pushing, packing,
Whew! Won't be back here until—When?

Next week.

The Gardener

David Rowbotham

I watched my father digging in his garden.
His spade, with a sound like the palm of a huge hand
Against a huger tree, struck through the soil,
Lifted, turned, let fall. He pounded with care
Each stubborn clod and broke it into earth
That flowed between his fingers;
And the peewit came from the nest in the camphor-laurel
And, with a bird's simplicity, like a child's trust,
Stabbed for worms in the shadow of his knees.
You cannot know the kindness of a man
Till you see him in a garden with a spade
And birds about his feet.

Mothers Come Flying

Anonymous

If you have bags,
Baskets, kids and prams,
It's not that easy
on buses and trams.

Mothers are ace at it,
They set a pace at it,
Bundling and shoving and folding,
Swaying and swinging and holding.
And you should watch,
At their stop,
Mothers and babies
On the hop.
Bags and baskets kids and prams
Mothers come flying
Off buses and trams.

Profiles of My Father

Rhyll McMaster

I

The night we went to see the Brisbane River
break its banks
my mother from her kitchen corner
stood on one foot and wailed, 'Oh Bill,
it's *dangerous.*'
'Darl,' my father reasoned,
'don't be Uncle Willy,'

And took me right down to the edge
at South Brisbane, near the Gasworks,
the Austin's small insignia winking
in the rain.

A policeman helped a man load
a mattress on his truck.
At a white railing we saw the brown water
boil off into the dark.
It rolled midstream higher than its banks
and people cheered when a cat on a crate,
and a white fridge whizzed past.

II

Every summer morning at five-thirty in the dark
I rummaged for my swimming bag
among musty gym shoes and Mum's hats from 1940
in the brown hail cupboard.
And Dad and I purred down through the sweet, fresh morning
Sill cool, but getting rosy
at Paul's Ice Cream factory,
and turned left at the Gasworks for South Brisbane Baths.

The day I was knocked off my kickboard
by an aspiring Olympian aged ten
it was cool and quiet and green down on the bottom.
Above the swaying ceiling limbs like pink logs,
and knifing arms churned past.
I looked at a crack in the cream wall
as I descended and thought of nothing.

When all of a sudden
Dad's legs, covered in silver bubbles,
his khaki shorts and feet in thongs
plunged into view like a new aquatic animal.
I was happy driving home;
Dad in a borrowed shirt with red poinsettias
and the Coach's light blue, shot-silk togs.

Glenelg

Jim Haynes

Glenelg puts a smile on my face,

With the sea and the sun and the space.

Wish it was my home,

It's a fine palindrome.

Spelled backward it's still the same place.

Night Noises

Patricia Wrightson

Who's there at my window? Who's that?
Who is walking as soft as a cat
In the dark of the night?

Now it's gone—the soft paw in the grass
Or the moth-wing that happened to pass.
I have put out the light.

Full Moon

Robin Klein

At times of full moon
(I wish I knew why)
I get this strange yearning
to howl at the sky!

For reasons peculiar
I've not yet discovered,
the backs of my hands then
with fur become covered!

My fingernails lengthen,
my hands look like paws!
I feel a compulsion
to walk on all fours!

My eyes redly glimmer,
hair sprouts from my ears.
Fang-like my teeth grow,
with points sharp as spears!

Though normally fussy
about what I eat,
on nights when the moon's full,
I crave *raw red meat!*

Nightening

Michael Dugan

When you wake up at night
And it's dark and frightening,
Climb out of bed
And turn on the lightening.

Things That Go Squark

Peter Wesley-Smith

There are things that go squark in the day-time,

There are things that go garkling at dawn;

There are things that gruffoon

In the late afternoon

Or whenever the curtains are drawn.

There are things that go swoosh in the morning,

There are things that enfooble and fight;

Ev'ry ev'ning at dusk

There are things quite grotusque,

There are things that go bump in the night.

There are things that go squelch in the spring-time,

There are things that go flark in the fall—

But the worst of the breed

Is a terror indeed:

It's a thing that goes nothing at all …

Sitting on the Fence

Michael Leunig

'Come sit down beside me,'
I said to myself,
And although it doesn't make sense,
I held my own hand
As a small sign of trust
And together I sat on the fence.

Free Wheeling on a Bike

Robert Gray

Freewheeling on a bike—
the butterflies of sunlight
all over me.

The Man from Ironbark

A.B. (Banjo) Paterson

It was the man from Ironbark who struck the Sydney town,

He wandered over street and park, he wandered up and down.

He loitered here, he loitered there, till he was like to drop,

Until at last in sheer despair he sought a barber's shop.

'Ere shave my beard and whiskers off, I'll be a man of mark,

I'll go and do the Sydney toff up home in Ironbark.'

The barber man was small and flash, as barbers mostly are,

He wore a strike-your-fancy sash, he smoked a huge cigar;

He was a humorist of note and keen at repartee,

He laid the odds and kept a 'tote', whatever that may be.

And when he saw our friend arrive, he whispered, 'Here's a lark!

Just watch me catch him all alive, this man from Ironbark.'

There were some gilded youths that sat along the barber's wall,

Their eyes were dull, their heads were flat, they had no brains at all;

To them the barber passed the wink, his dexter eyelid shut,

'I'll make this bloomin' yokel think his bloomin' throat is cut.'

And as he soaped and rubbed it in he made a rude remark:

'I s'pose the flats is pretty green up there in Ironbark.'

A grunt was all reply he got; he shaved the bushman's chin,
Then made the water boiling hot and dipped the razor in.
He raised his hand, his brow grew black, he paused a while to gloat,
Then slashed the red-hot razor-back across his victim's throat;
Upon the newly-shaven skin it made a livid mark—
No doubt it fairly took him in—the man from Ironbark.

He fetched a wild up-country yell might wake the dead to hear,
And though his throat, he knew full well, was cut from ear to ear,
He struggled gamely to his feet, and faced the murd'rous foe:
'You've done for me! you dog, I'm beat! one hit before I go!
I only wish I had a knife, you blessed murdering shark!
But you'll remember all your life the man from Ironbark.'

He lifted up his hairy paw, with one tremendous clout
He landed on the barber's jaw, and knocked the barber out
He set to work with nail and tooth, he made the place a wreck;
He grabbed the nearest gilded youth, and tried to break his neck.
And all the while his throat he held to save his vital spark,
And 'Murder! Bloody Murder!' yelled the man from Ironbark.

A peeler man who heard the din came in to see the show;
He tried to run the bushman in, but he refused to go.
And when at last the barber spoke, and said ''Twas all in fun—
'Twas just a little harmless joke, a trifle overdone.'
'A joke!' he cried. 'By George, that's fine; a lively sort of lark;
I'd like to catch that murdering swine some night in Ironbark.'

And now while round the shearing floor the list'ning shearers gape,
He tells the story o'er and o'er, and brags of his escape.
'Them barber chaps what keeps a tote, by George, I've had enough,
One tried to cut my bloomin' throat, but thank the Lord it's tough.'
And whether he's believed or no, there's one thing to remark,
That flowing beards are all the go way up in Ironbark.

The Wagtail

Judith Wright

So elegant he is and neat
from round black head to slim black feet!
He sways and flirts upon the fence,
His collar clean as innocence.

The city lady looks and cries,
'Oh charming bird with dewdrop eyes,
How kind of you to sing that song!'
But what a pity—she is wrong.

'Sweet pretty creature'—yes, but who
is the one that he sings to?

Not me – not you.

The furry moth, the gnat perhaps,
on which his scissor-beak snip-snaps.

Peacocks

Kate Llewellyn

On wet days
they hang on the verandah railing
like wet curtains
the peahens
become grey cushions
that fell in a river

but on dry days
celebration
shimmer and tremble
shake that castanet
the Spanish dance begins

up goes the opera set
raised as if a cord were pulled
or a child's stand-up picture book
opened

their strong grey legs
strut and hawk this show
around the farm
from town to town

and the singing
so gruesome
it were best left to others
however
like Cinderella's sisters
no-one dares mention
such ugliness to them
while the little plain butcher bird
sings so ravishingly
sitting almost unnoticed on a post

One Return

Nicolette Stasko

Needles of the casuarinas
are pale green hair

white cockatoos
in the trees

like sheets of paper
clean handkerchiefs

unfolding in the wind
all is silent

except the rumbling
of the train past

two old men on dry grass
basking in the sun

seagulls lost
in a grey parking lot

a half eaten melon—
rind of last night's moon

leaves turn purple
in the falling dusk

the train
rumbles on

everything held together
by an eye

From The Call of the City

Victor Daley

There is a saying of renown—
'God made the country, man the town.'
Well, everybody to his trade!
But man likes best the thing he made.
The town has little space to spare;
The country has both space and air;
The town's confined, the country's free—
Yet, spite of all, the town for me.

For when the hills are grey and night is falling,
      And the winds sigh drearily,
I hear the city calling, calling, calling,
      With a voice like the great sea.

Part 5

All Along the River:
To the Sea

The Beach

William Hart-Smith

The beach is a quarter of golden fruit,

a soft ripe melon

sliced to a half-moon curve,

having a thick green rind

of jungle growth;

and the sea devours it

with its sharp,

sharp white teeth.

The Sea

Lilith Norman

Deep glass-green seas
chew rocks
with their green-glass jaws.
But little waves
creep in
and nibble softly at the sand.

Shark

Geoffrey Dutton

Sometimes when the shallow water is clear and green
A long and steadily moving shape is seen,
And the whole bright bay suddenly grows dark,
And swimmers rush for the shore at the cry of 'Shark!'

Porpoises bounce cheerfully up and down
But sharks go grimly straight, as if a frown
Was above the horrible grin I cannot see,
And those little eyes were glaring straight at me.

Lazily the dark shape turns, to disappear
Above the weed, and the sea is full of fear.
No thank you, just now I haven't any wish
To swim, or even to launch the boat to fish.

The Sunbather

John Thompson

I shield my face. My eyes are closed. I spin
With nearing sleep. I am dissolved within
Myself, and softened like a ripening fruit.
I swing in a red-hazy void, I sway
With tides of blind heat. From a far-off sphere,
Like scratchings on a pillow, voices I hear
And thundering waves and thuds of passing feet;
For there, out there beyond me, lads and girls
In dazzling colours and with gleaming skin
Through sands of gold and surfs of opal run;
They dive beneath the long green claw which curls
Above them; on the white comber they shoot
Shoreward; many in a slow spiral melt
Like me into oblivion under the sun.

Diver

R.A. Simpson

Alone on the tower
I'm not confident.
The water is black
And distant.

I think of style
And raise my arms and aim,
Holding back the plunge.
It's mostly a game

That touches terror,
Then terror goes—
I view my fingers,
My toes.

'Defiance, love and revolt
Make the diver dive
And prove, through dying,
He's alive,'
A voice preaches in my head…

And so I dive.

Water gulps me down,
Chilling me with its grip,
Then arms pine up and up
Like worship.

The Rock Pool

Peter Skryznecki

The rock pool
is a magic circle
full of colours the sea
washes in—
blues, greens, browns, reds:
yellow that leaps
in reflection
and does a somersault
over your head!
Seagrass weaves
in slow, soft dances—
reaches up to your face
and hands:
growing out of tiny pebbles
and the patterns
of drifting sand.
Here's a crab
that scuttles sideways,
hiding under a shelf of stone.

Look—here's a fish
with purple stripes!
And—there—
a piece of cuttlebone.
The rock pool
is a magic circle
full of treasures
from a sea king's cave—
thrown up for the delight
of children
by swirling tide
and crashing waves!

Tide Talk

Max Fatchen

The tide and I had stopped to chat
About the waves where seabirds sat,
About the yachts with bobbing sails
And quite enormous, spouting whales.

The tide has lots to talk about.
Sometimes it's in. Sometimes it's out.
For something you must understand,
It's up and down across the sand;
Sometimes it's low and sometimes high,
It's very wet and never dry.

The tide, quite crossly, said: 'The sea
Is always out there pushing me.
And just when I am feeling slack,
It sends me in then drags me back.
It never seems to let me go.
I rise. I fall. I'm to and fro.'

I told the tide, 'I know it's true

For I am pushed around like you.

And really do they think it's fair?

Do this. Do that. Come here. Go there.'

Then loudly came my parents' shout.

So I went in.

    The tide went out.

Dolphins

Peter McFarlane

Piano, violin and cello dance gently
claiming the airspace of the shack
now open to the blueness of sea
and the light of late morning.
Heat rises outside,
catches wandering butterflies in its shimmer.
I look out over the fringe of dunes
searching for dolphins,
waiting for them to appear suddenly,
as they always do,
like scattered crotchets and quavers
strung out across sandbars
and the slow swell of waves.
They always come,
dorsal fins like flags,
bodies glistening brown
with the sheen of rocks when waves subside,
sometimes as close as the yellow-winged honeyeaters
dipping beaks into the wells of flowers
outside my window. Once
I stood knee-deep in surf,

heels sucking back into sand,

as dolphins squinnied on the backs of waves

and kidded that I join them.

A power boat crosses the bay

making waves where there are none;

dry grasses and stiffened brown stalks

stir restlessly on the dunes;

more power boats cross the horizon

trailing white trains of foam.

The trio start their final movement,

allegro maestoso.

I look to the sea.

I know they will come.

If I keep looking I know the dolphins will come,

claim the sea as their own

and be gone.

A Wind from the Sea

Randolph Stow

Wind that breaks across the bay
tumbles the grass in green and grey.

Lapped by grass, with posts alean,
the house patchpeels in grey and green.

High up in those blistered walls
a window lifts, some dimness falls.

Loosed into the weather, grey
tatters of lacework suck and splay.

Past those curtains lies a room.
Almond-husks bear such grey bloom.

In that room some figure stands:
brushing a greyness from its hands.

Holding back the bellying lace.
Wind, salt wind, across its face.

Part 6

All Along the River: Horizon and Beyond

Epiphany

Dorothy Hewett

a day like this
both dark and bright
with cloud
loudness of water
and found words …

the sky no longer
at the top
nor the ground
under my feet
I am lifted up
into a shaft of light
pointed like a sword …

unknown island
neither night
nor day
but furious noise
luminous universe
between the black crags
and the running sea

this was the place.

Trails

Eva Johnson

I once walked along the trails of my ancestors
through deserts, mountains, rivers and sands
where food was plenty,
where goanna tracks led to waterholes
where the bandicoot whistled its name.
I gathered nuts from the kurrajong tree
and suckled wild honey.
I swam with catfish in billabongs of waterlilies
and tasted cooked food from ovens underground.
I smelled the promise of the winds
along trails of the dreaming
and traced my mother's footsteps embedded in the sand.

I once walked along the trails of my ancestors
that now have blown away with the winds of time.
Only in memory will I walk along the trails
Only in memory will they remain.

Kingsford-Smith

Winifred Tennant

Ask the sun; it has watched him pass—
A shadow mirrored on seas of glass;
Ask the stars that he knew so well
If they beheld where a bird-man fell.
Ask the wind that has blown with him
Over the edge of the ocean's rim,
Far from the charted haunts of men,
To the utmost limits and back again.
Ask the clouds on the mountain height,
The echoes that followed him in his flight,
The thunder that prowls the midnight sky,
If a silvered 'plane went riding by.

If the birds could talk, would they tell the fall
Of a god who winged above them all?
Of an eagle man, by the world's decrees,
King of the blue immensities?

Eclipse of the Moon

Elizabeth Riddell

This is a profitable night, the moon's eclipse
at last a reason for not sleeping.
There is a reason to wake every hour
to observe the shape and size of door and window
and wall and picture frame,
turn on the lamp, open the book
and let it fall away, reason to rise, make tea,
pad to the door,
stand on cool tiles
to watch the invaded moon.
I see a jagged one third of her beauty left
and somewhere, black layers back,
a rim of light.

Sometimes the moon strays into daytime skies
Ophelia-wan.
Tonight she was glittering and wild
until the mask slid down,
erasing all her gold.

The Australian Sunrise

James Lister Cuthbertson

The Morning Star paled slowly, the Cross hung low to the sea,

And down the shadowy reaches the tide came swirling free,

The lustrous purple blackness of the soft Australian night,

Waned in the grey awakening that heralded the light;

Still in the dying darkness, still in the forest dim

The pearly dew of the dawning clung to each giant limb,

Till the sun came up from the ocean, red with the cold sea mist,

And smote on the limestone ridges, and the shining tree-tops kissed;

Then the fiery Scorpion vanished, the magpie's note was heard,

And the wind in the she-oak wavered and the honeysuckles stirred;

The airy golden vapour rose from the river breast,

The kingfisher came darting out of his crannied nest,

And the bulrushes and reed-beds put off their sallow grey

And burnt with cloudy crimson at the dawning of the day.

The Star Tribes

Fred Biggs

Look, among the boughs. Those stars are men.
There's Ngintu, with his dogs, who guards the skins
of Everlasting Water in the sky.
And there's the Crow-man, carrying on his back
the wounded Hawk-man. There's the serpent, Thurroo,
glistening in the leaves. There's Kapeetah,
the Moon-man, sitting in his mia-mia.

And there's those Seven Sisters, travelling
across the sky. They make the real cold frost.
You hear them when you're camped out on the plains.
They look down from the sky and see your fire
and 'Mai, mai, mai,' they'd sing out as they run
across the sky. And, when you wake, you find
your swag, the camp, the plains, all white with frost.

No Point in Staying Up Longer

David Brooks

No point in staying up longer,
thoughts all sad and astray,
the Six Beautiful Sisters
sound asleep long ago,
and the seventh away, Orion
gone off with his goats somewhere
and the Great Bear sleeping,
Castor and Pollux and Aldebaran
so far up in the mountains now
no-one is calling them home.

The People

John Tranter

The people come down from the hills
In the evening. We greet them.
Woodsmoke follows the valley,
It is the quiet time of the year.

We walk with them a short way
For we shall not see them again.
They will pass over the ocean
Hoping for nothing, receiving the sky
And we shall continue in the valley
From spring to autumn, planting
And reaping, and in the blue winter night
Dreaming of the gentle people who departed.

Song of the Yellow

John Shaw Neilson

How shall a poor man sing
When all the birds compete?
With young Love scarlet ripe
'O yellow, yellow sweet!
They have come out to pipe:
O yellow, yellow, yellow, yellow, yellow, yellow sweet!'

How shall a cool man sing?
He shall not find the heat;
These foresters take up
Gold of the honey-cup,
And chime on 'Yellow sweet!
O yellow, yellow, yellow, yellow, yellow, yellow sweet!'

The impatient apricot
Says, 'Now remember not
Songs of a sorrow, sing
Loud to each living thing
Here in the loving heat:
O yellow, yellow, yellow, yellow, yellow, yellow sweet!'

How shall a dull man sing?

Shall he the darkness cheat?

The birds to heaven climb

In the full summer-time

And cry on 'Yellow sweet!

O yellow, yellow, yellow, yellow, yellow, yellow sweet!'

Be Content

Christopher Brennan

The point of noon is past, outside: light is asleep;
brooding upon its perfect hour: the woods are deep
and solemn, fill'd with unseen presences of light
that glint, allure, and hide them; ever yet more bright
(it seems) the turn of a path will show them: nay, but rest;
seek not, and think not; dream, and know not; this is best:
the hour is full; be lost: whispering, the woods are bent,
This is the only revelation; be content.

About Libby Hathorn

Libby Hathorn has had a lifelong love affair with poetry. She finds it a continual source of inspiration in her work and in her life, with many of her stories beginning with fragments of poetry. Libby has won awards and commendations for her novels and picture books for young people, several of which have been adapted into movies, plays and opera. She is currently working on a fantasy novel and her arts program 100 Views (100views.com.au), bringing poetry to schools and especially to teachers, in Australia and overseas.

To find out more information about Libby Hathorn, visit her website at libbyhathorn.com.

Sources

Anonymous, excerpt from 'Bold Jack Donahoe'. This nineteenth-century ballad came to represent an enduring popular perception of Australian bushrangers. Donahoe is acknowledged as the likely originator for the more popular and widely distributed ballad, 'The Wild Colonial Boy'.

Anonymous, excerpt from 'Click Go the Shears'. First published in an article by Percy Jones for *Twentieth Century*, vol. 1, no. 1, 1946. Later published in *Old Bush Songs*, Douglas Stewart and Nancy Keesing (editors), Angus & Robertson, Sydney, 1957.

Anonymous, 'Drought', retitled 'How Long, Oh Lord!' in *An Anthology of Australian Poetry to 1920*, Part III, John Kinsella (editor), University of Western Australia, 2007.

Anonymous, 'Ned Kelly Song', from *Four Corners: An Anthology of Poetry*, A.K. Thomson (editor), Jacaranda Press, Brisbane, 1987.

Anonymous, excerpt from 'The Old Bullock Dray', from A.B. Paterson (editor) *The Old Bush Songs*, Angus & Robertson, Sydney, 1906.

Fred Biggs (1875–1961), 'The Star Tribes' by Fred Biggs, from R. Robinson (compiling editor), *Aljteringa and other Aboriginal Poems*, published by A.W. and A.H. Reed, Sydney, 1970. Reproduced by permission of New Holland Publishers.

Christopher Brennan (1870–1932), 'Be Content', from *Poems 1913*, Angus & Robertson, Sydney, 1992.

David Brooks (b. 1953), 'No Point in Staying Up Longer', unpublished poem. Reproduced courtesy of Tim Curnow Literary Agent and Consultant, Sydney.

David Campbell (1915–1979), 'On Frosty Days', from *Selected Poems 1942-1968*, Angus & Robertson, Sydney, 1968. Reproduced by permission of *HarperCollins*Publishers.

James Cuthbertson (1851–1910), 'The Australian Sunrise' and 'The Bush', first published in *Barwon Ballads*, George Robertson & Company, Melbourne, 1893.

Victor Daley (1858–1905), excerpt from 'The Call of the City', from Bertram Stevens (editor), *Wine and Roses*, Angus & Robertson, Sydney, 1911.

C.J. Dennis (1876–1938), excerpt from 'A Song of Rain', first published in *Backblock Ballads and Later Verses*, Angus & Robertson, Sydney, 1918.

Michael Dugan (1947–2006), 'Dilemma', from *Poetry Alive*, Elaine Hamilton (editor), Hodder Education, 1976. Reproduced by permission of Sally Dugan.
    'Nightening', from *100 Australian Poems for Children*, Clare Scott-Mitchell and Kathlyn Griffith (editors), Random House Australia, Sydney, 2002. Reproduced by permission of Sally Dugan.

Mary Duroux (b. 1934), 'I Am', first published in *Dirge by Hidden Art*, Heritage Publishing, Moruya, NSW, 1992. Reproduced by permission of the author.

Geoffrey Dutton (1922–1998), 'Shark', from *On My Island*, F.W. Cheshire, Melbourne, 1967. Reproduced by arrangement with the licensor, The Estate of Geoffrey Dutton, through Curtis Brown (Aust) Pty Ltd.

Edward Dyson (1865–1931), excerpt from 'The Old Whim Horse', from *Rhymes from the Mines*, Angus & Robertson, Sydney, 1896.

Max Fatchen (b. 1920), 'Tide Talk', from *A Paddock of Poems*, Omnibus/Puffin, Adelaide, 1987. Copyright © Max Fatchen. Reproduced by permission of Johnson & Alcock Ltd.
    'Old Horses', from *A Pocketful of Rhymes*, Omnibus Books, Adelaide, 1989. Copyright © Max Fatchen. Reproduced by permission of Johnson & Alcock Ltd.

John Foulcher (b. 1952), 'The Glasshouse Mountains', from *Honeymoon Snaps*, Angus & Robertson, Sydney, 1956. Reproduced by permission of *HarperCollins*Publishers.

Mary Gilmore (1865–1962), 'The Great Snake', from *The Singing Tree*, Angus & Robertson, Sydney, 1971. Reproduced courtesy of the publishers, ETT Imprint.

Robert Gray (b. 1945), excerpt from 'The Dusk', from *Glass Script*, Angus & Robertson, Sydney, 1979. Reproduced by permission of Margaret Connolly & Associates.

'Free Wheeling on a Bike', from *Creewater Journal*, University of Queensland Press, St Lucia, 1974. Reproduced by permission of Margaret Connolly & Associates.

Mary Hannay Foott (1846–1918), 'Where the Pelican Builds Her Nest' and excerpt from 'In Time of Drought', first published in *Where the Pelican Builds, and other Poems*, Gordon and Gotch, Brisbane, 1885.

Kevin Hart (b. 1954), 'A Tree' by Kevin Hart, unpublished poem. Reproduced by permission of the author.

William Hart-Smith (1911–1990), 'The Beach' and 'Tractor', from *Birds, Beasts and Flowers*, Puffin, 1996. Reproduced by Penguin Group (Australia).

Gwen Harwood (1920–1995), 'Crow-Call', from *Selected Poems*, Gregory Kratzmann (editor), Penguin Books Australia, Melbourne, 2001. Reproduced by permission of Penguin Group (Australia).

Libby Hathorn (b. 1943), 'Mothers Come Flying', 'Rainforest Song', 'Supermarket' and 'Tree Australia Tree' and from *Talks with my Skateboard*, ABC Books, 1991. Reproduced by kind permission of the author.

Jim Haynes, 'Glenelg', from *An Australian Treasury of Popular Verses*, ABC Books, Sydney, 2002. Reproduced by permission of the author.

Steven Herrick (b. 1958), 'The Big River', from *By the River*, Allen & Unwin, Sydney, 2004.

Dorothy Hewett (1923–2002), 'Epiphany', from *Peninsula*, Fremantle Arts Centre Press, South Fremantle, WA, 1994.

Henry Kendall (1839–1882), 'Bell Birds', from *The Poems of Henry Kendall*, Angus & Robertson, Sydney, 1920.

Robin Klein (1936–2004) 'Full Moon', from *Snakes and Ladders*, J.M. Dent (Houghton Mifflin Australia), Melbourne, 1985. Reproduced by arrangement with the licensor, Robin Klein, through Curtis Brown (Aust) Pty Ltd.

Eva Johnson (b. 1946), 'Uluru' and 'Trails' from *Differences: Writings by Women*, Susan Hawthorne (editor), Waterloo Press, Sydney, 1985. Reproduced by permission of Eva Johnson.

J. Andrew Johnstone, excerpt from 'Mullumbimby to Bondi Beach', unpublished poem. Reproduced by kind permission of the author.

Henry Lawson (1867–1922), excerpt from 'The Never-Never Land', first published in *Joe Wilson and His Mates*, Blackwood, Edinburgh-London, 1901. Published in *Poetical Works of Henry Lawson*, Angus & Robertson, Sydney, 1925.

'Andy's Gone with Cattle' and 'Ballad of the Drover', first published in *In the Days When the World was Wide*, Angus & Robertson, Sydney, 1896.

'In Possum Land', first published in *For Australia and Other Poems*, Standard publishing, Melbourne, 1913.

'On the Night Train', first published in *Birth*, Vol 6, No. 64, March 1922. Later published in *Winnowed Verses*, Angus & Robertson, Sydney, 1942.

'The Days when we went Swimming' by Henry Lawson, first published in *Verses Popular and Humorous*, Angus & Robertson, Sydney, 1900.

'Trouble on the Selection', first published by his mother L. Lawson in *Short Stories in Prose and Verse*, 1894. Later published in *Verse Popular and Humorous*, Angus & Robertson, Sydney, 1900 *Poetical Works of Henry Lawson*, Angus & Robertson, 1918.

Michael Leunig (b. 1945), 'Sitting on the Fence', from *Short notes from the long history of happiness*, Penguin Books Australia, Melbourne, 1996. Reproduced by permission of Penguin Group (Australia).

Kate Llewellyn (b. 1940), 'Peacocks', from her collection *Figs*, Hudson Publishing, 1990. Reproduced courtesy of Tim Curnow Literary Agent and Consultant, Sydney.

Dorothea Mackellar (1885–1968), 'My Country', first published as 'Core of My Heart' in 1908. Reproduced by arrangement with the licensor, The Estate of Dorothea Mackellar, through Curtis Brown (Aust) Pty Ltd.

Doug MacLeod (b. 1959), 'The Bunyips', first published in Jane Covernton (compiling editor), *Petrifying Poems*, Omnibus Books, Adelaide, 1986. Reproduced by permission of the author.

Hugh McCrae (1876–1958), 'Song of the Rain', from *Poems*, Angus & Robertson, Sydney, 1939. Reproduced by permission of *HarperCollins*Publishers.

Peter McFarlane (b. 1940), 'Dolphins', from Sarah Keane (compiling editor), *It Must Have Been Summer*, Oxford University Press, Melbourne, 1990. Reproduced by arrangement with the licensor, Peter McFarlane, through Curtis Brown (Aust) Pty Ltd.

Rhyll McMaster (b. 1947), 'Tanks', from *The Brineshrimp*, University of Queensland Press, Brisbane, 1972. Reproduced by permission of the author.
— 'Profiles of My Father', first published in *Washing the Money*, Angus & Robertson, 1986. Reproduced by permission of the author.

Jack Moses (1861–1945),'Nine Miles from Gundagai', from *Nine Miles from Gundagai*, Angus & Robertson, Sydney, 1938.

Les A. Murray (b. 1938), 'Rainwater Tank', from *Ethnic Radio*, Angus & Robertson, Sydney, 1977. Also published in *The Vernacular Republic Poems 1961-1981*, Angus & Robertson, Sydney, 1982. Reproduced by permission of Margaret Connolly & Associates.

John Shaw Neilson (1872–1942), 'Song of the Yellow', from James Devaney (editor), *Unpublished Poems of Shaw Neilsen*, Angus & Robertson, Sydney, 1947.

Gela Nga-Mirraitja (Fordham) (c.1930s–2006), excerpt from 'The Law About Singing Out', from 'Talking History', *Land Rights* News 2, 9 July 1988. Reproduced by permission of Northern Land Council.

Lilith Norman (b. 1927), 'The Sea', from Jonah Foster (editor), *Another First Poetry Book*, Oxford University Press, USA, 1988. Reproduced by permission of Margaret Connolly & Associates.

John O'Brien (1878–1952), 'Said Hanrahan', from *Around the Boree Log*, Angus & Robertson, Sydney, 1921.

Mark O'Connor (b. 1945), 'Clinging', from *Poetry of the Mountains*, Second Back Row Press, Leura, NSW, 1988. Reproduced by arrangement with the licensor, Mark O'Connor through Curtis Brown (Aust) Pty Ltd.

Oodgeroo of the Tribe Noonuccal (Kath Walker) (1920–1993), 'The Bunyip', from *My People*, 4th edition, John Wiley & Sons Australia, Ltd, 2008. Reproduced by permission of John Wiley & Sons Australia, Ltd.

A.B. (Banjo) Paterson (1864–1941), excerpt from 'Waltzing Matilda', from *The Collected Verse of A.B. Paterson*, Angus & Robertson, Sydney, 1921. Reproduced by permission of Retrusa Pty Ltd.

'Clancy of the Overflow', first published in *The Man From Snowy River and Other Verses*, Angus & Robertson, Sydney, 1895.

'The Man from Snowy River', from *The Collected Verse of A.B. Paterson*, Angus & Robertson, Sydney, 1921. Reproduced by permission of Retrusa Pty Ltd.

Grace Perry (1927–1987), 'Face of the City', from A.K. Thompson (editor), *The Four Corners: an Anthology of Poetry*, The Jacaranda Press, 1968. Reproduced by kind permission of John Millett.

Roderic Quinn (1867–1949), 'The Song of Cicadas' by Roderic Quinn, from *An Australian Heritage of Verse*, Jim Haynes (compiling editor), ABC Books, 2000. Reproduced by permission of Jim Haynes.

Elizabeth Riddell (1909–1998), 'Eclipse of the Moon', from *From the Midnight Courtyard*, Angus & Robertson, Sydney, 1989. Reproduced by permission of *HarperCollins*Publishers.

Archie Roach (b. 1956), excerpt from 'Took the Children Away'. Written by Archie Roach (Mushroom Music Publishing). Reprinted with permission.

J.M. Roache (b. 1917), 'When the Golden Grain is Ripe', unpublished poem. Reproduced with kind permission of the author.

David Rowbotham (b. 1924), 'The Gardener', from A.K. Thompson (editor), *The Four Corners: an Anthology of Poetry*, The Jacaranda Press, 1968. Reproduced by permission of the author.

Bill Scott (1923–2005), 'Frogs', from *See What I've Got'*, the Bill Scott Reciter series, Triple D Books, Wagga Wagga, NSW, 2001. Reproduced by permission of Mavis Scott.

Thomas Shapcott (b. 1935), 'In the Forest', from *The Mankind Thing*, Jacaranda Press, Brisbane, 1964. Reproduced by permission of the author.

R.A. Simpson (1929–2002) 'Diver', from *Selected Poems*, University of Queensland Press, St Lucia, 1981. Reproduced by kind permission of Pam Simpson.

Peter Skryznecki (b. 1945), 'The Rock Pool', from Jill Heylen and Celia Jellett (editors) *Someone is Flying Balloons*, Omnibus Books, Adelaide, 1983.

Nicolette Stasko (b. 1950), 'One Return', from *The Weight of Irises*, Black Pepper Publishing, Melbourne, 2003. Reproduced by permission of Black Pepper Publishing.

Randolph Stow (1935–1979), 'A Wind from the Sea', from *Selected Poems: A Counterfeit Silence*, Angus & Robertson Publishers, Sydney, 1969. Copyright © Randolph Stow 1969. Reproduced by permission of Sheil Land Associates Ltd.

Winifred Tennant, 'Kingsford-Smith', from Jim Haynes and Jillian Dellit, *Great Australian Aviation Stories*, ABC Books, Sydney, 2006. Reproduced by permission of Jim Haynes.

John Thompson (1907–1968), 'The Sunbather', from Jill Bryant, *Australian Visions*, Hodder Education, Sydney, 1996. Reproduced with permission of Peter Thompson.

John Tranter (b. 1943) 'The People' by John Tranter, unpublished poem. Reproduced courtesy of Australian Literary Management.

Peter Wesley-Smith (b. 1942) 'Things That Go Squark', first published in Jane Covernton (compiling editor) *Petrifying Poems*, Omnibus Books, 1986. Reproduced by permission of the author.

Judith Wright (1915–2000), 'Parrots' and 'The Wagtail', from *Birds: Poems by Judith Wright*, Angus & Robertson, Sydney, 1962. © Meredith McKinney. National Library of Australia, 2000. Reproduced by permission of *HarperCollins*Publishers.

Patricia Wrightson (b. 1921), 'Night Noises', from *A First Australian Poetry Book*, Oxford University Press, Melbourne, 1983. Reproduced by arrangement with the licensor, Patricia Wrightson, through Curtis Brown (Aust) Pty Ltd.

Index of First Lines

Across the stony ridges, 152

a day like this 166

A kangaroo is standing up, and dwindling like a plant 101

Alone on the tower 152

Ask the sun; it has watched him pass— 168

At Murray Bridge the bunyips wait 38

At times of full moon— 128

By channels of coolness the echoes are calling, 30

By hut, homestead, and shearing-shed, 50

'Come sit down beside me,' 132

Coolangatta 24

Deep glass-green seas 149

Dragging an iron rake 100

Empty rings when tapped give tongue, 88

Fat frogs squat greenly 96

Freewheeling on a bike— 133

Give us from dawn to dark 33

Glenelg puts a smile on my face, 126

Have you seen the bush by moonlight, from the train, go running by? 78

He's an old grey horse, with his head bowed sadly, 92

Hey, bottlebrush you! 112

How shall a poor man sing 174

I am 20

I had written him a letter which I had, for want of better 106

I once walked along the trails of my ancestors 167

I shield my face. My eyes are closed. I spin 151

I watched my father digging in his garden. 122

I will see you in November 84

I've done my share of shearing sheep, 80

If you have bags, 123

In Possum Land the night are fair, 69

Into a hole into the ground he went, 97

Isolated rock, 68

It takes a life to understand a tree. 110

It was the man from Ironbark who struck the Sydney town, 134

Let this be eternal life: 64

Look, among the boughs. Those stars are men. 171

Loquats are cold as winter suns. 63

Mullumbimby, Moree, 25

My father used to do it. We used to get up early in the morning 74

Ned Kelly was born in a ramshackle hut, 42

Needles of the casuarinas 140

Night, 86

No point in staying up longer, 172

Now the shearing is all over, and the wool is coming down 54

Oh don't bring down 37

Oh there once was a swagman camped in the Billabongs. 56

Old horses, 90

On frosty days, when I was young, 79

On wet days 138

Our Andy's gone with cattle now— 108

Out on the board the old shearer stands, 51

Patter, patter . . . Boolcoonatta, 21

Piano, violin and cello dance gently 158

So elegant he is and neat   137

Sometimes when the shallow water is clear and green 150

The beach is a quarter of golden fruit, 148

The big river 22

The breezes waved the silver grass, 82

The freeway 66

The horses were ready, the rails were down, 94

The love of field and coppice 75

The Morning Star paled slowly, the Cross hung low to the sea, 170

The night we went to see the Brisbane River 124

The people come down from the hills 173

The point of noon is past, outside: light is asleep; 176

The rock pool 154

The rushes are black by the river bed, 48

The tide and I had stopped to chat 156

There are things that go squark in the day-time, 131

There is a saying of renown— 142

There was movement at the station, for the word had passed around 58

There's the jingle and the jangle 121

They are changing the face of the city; 120

This is a profitable night, the moon's eclipse 169

This story's right, the story's true 114

To cling, by a breaking fingernail, to an undercut cliff, 36

Travelling, 87

'Twas of a valiant highwayman and outlaw of disdain 40

Wait for the axe sound in the forest. 34

Wearily watching and waiting for rain, 49

'We'll all be rooned,' said Hanrahan, 43

When you wake up at night 130

Who's there at my window? Who's that? 127

Wind that breaks across the bay 160

Yesterday there came to me 98

You keep quiet now, little fella, 39

You lazy boy, you're here at last, 52

Index of Authors and Titles

Andy's Gone with Cattle, 108–109

Australian Sunrise, The, 170

Ballad of the Drover, 102–105

Be Content, 176

Beach, The, 148

Bell-Birds, 30–32

Big River, The, 22–23

Biggs, Fred, 171

Bold Jack Donahoe, 40–41

Brennan, Christopher, 176

Brooks, David, 172

Bunyip, The, 39

Bunyips, The, 38

Bush, The, 35

Call of the City, The, 142

Campbell, David, 79

Clancy of the Overflow, 106–107

Click Go the Shears, 51

Clinging, 36

Crow-Call, 64–65

Cuthbertson, James Lister, 35, 170

Daley, Victor, 142

Days When We Went Swimming, The,
    82–83

Dennis, C.J., 21

Dilemma, 24

Diver, 152–153

Dolphins, 158–159

Drought, 49

Dugan, Michael, 24, 130

Duroux, Mary, 20

Dusk, The, 101

Dutton, Geoffrey, 150

Dyson, Edward, 92–93

Eclipse of the Moon, 169

Epiphany, 166

Face of the City, 120

Fatchen, Max, 90–91, 156–157

Foulcher, John, 66–67

Free Wheeling on a Bike, 133

Frogs, 96

Full Moon, 128–129

Gardener, The, 122

Gilmore, Mary, 97

Glasshouse Mountains, The, 66–67

Glenelg, 126

Gray, Robert, 101, 135

Great Snake, The, 97

Hannay Foott, Mary, 48, 94–95

Hart, Kevin, 110–111

Hart-Smith, William, 100, 148

Harwood, Gwen, 64–65

Hathorn, Libby, 37, 112–113, 121, 123

Haynes, Jim, 126

Herrick, Steven, 22–23

Hewett, Dorothy, 166

I Am, 20

In Possum Land, 69

In the Forest, 34–3 5

In Time of Drought, 48

Johnson, Eva, 68, 167

Johnstone, J. Andrew, 25

Kendall, Henry, 30–32

Kingsford-Smith, 168

Klein, Robin, 128–129

Law About Singing Out, The, 74

Lawson, Henry, 50, 52–53, 69, 78, 82–83, 102–105, 108–109

Leunig, Michael, 132

Lister Cuthbertson, James

Llewellyn, Kate, 138–139

Mackellar, Dorothea, 75–77

MacLeod, Doug, 38

Man from Ironbark, The, 134–136

Man from Snowy River, The, 58–62

McCrae, Hugh, 86

McFarlane, Peter, 158–159

McMaster, Rhyll, 87, 124–125

Moses, Jack, 80–81

Mothers Come Flying, 123

Mullumbimby to Bondi Beach, 25

Murray, Les A., 88–89

My Country, 75–77

Ned Kelly Song, 42

Neilson, John Shaw, 174–175

Never-Never Land, The, 50

Nga-Mirraitja, Gela, 74

Night Noises, 127

Nightening, 130

Nine Miles from Gundagai, 80–81

No Point in Staying Up Longer, 172

Norman, Lilith, 149

O'Brien, John, 43–47

O'Connor, Mark, 36

Old Bullock Dray, The, 54–55

Old Horses, 90–91

Old Whim Horse, The, 92–93

On Frosty Days, 79

On the Night Train, 78

One Return, 140–141

Oodgeroo of the Tribe Noonuccal, 39

Parrots, 63

Paterson, A.B. (Banjo), 56–62, 106–107, 134–136

Peacocks, 138–139

People, The, 173

Perry, Grace, 120

Profiles of my Father, 124–125

Quinn, Roderic, 98–99

Rainforest Song, 37

Rainwater Tank, 88–89

Riddell, Elizabeth, 169

Roach, Archie, 114–115

Roache, J.M., 84–85

Rock Pool, The, 154–155

Rowbotham, David, 122

Said Hanrahan, 43–47

Scott, Bill, 96

Sea, The, 149

Shapcott, Thomas, 34–35

Shark, 150

Simpson, R.A., 152–153

Sitting on the Fence, 132

Skryznecki, Peter, 154–155

Song of Rain, A, 21

Song of the Cicadas, The, 98–99

Song of the Rain, 86

Song of the Yellow, 174–175

Star Tribes, The, 171

Stasko, Nicolette, 140–141

Stow, Randolph, 160–161

Sunbather, The, 151

Supermarket, 121

Tanks, 87

Tennant, Winifred, 168

Things that Go Squark, 131

Thompson, John, 151

Tide Talk, 156–157

Took the Children Away, 114–115

Tractor, 100

Trails, 167

Tranter, John, 173

Tree, A, 110–111

Tree Australia Tree, 112–113

Trouble on the Selection, 52–53

Uluru, 68

Wagtail, The, 137

Waltzing Matilda, 56–57

Wesley-Smith, Peter, 131

When the Golden Grain is Ripe, 84–85

Where the Pelican Builds Her Nest, 94–95

Wind from the Sea, A, 160–161

Wright, Judith, 65, 137

Wrightson, Patricia, 127